The Sandbag Secret

Stories linking with the History
National Curriculum Key Stage 2

First published in 1997 by Franklin Watts
338 Euston Road, London NW1 3BH

Franklin Watts Australia
Level 17/207 Kent Street, Sydney NSW 2000

This edition published 2002
Text © Jon Blake 1997

Editor: Kyla Barber
Designer: Jason Anscomb
Consultant: Dr Anne Millard, BA Hons, Dip Ed, PhD

A CIP catalogue record for this book
is available from the British Library.

ISBN 978 0 7496 4603 5

Dewey Classification 943.086

Printed in Great Britain

Franklin Watts is a division of Hachette Children's Books,
an Hachette Livre UK company.
www.hachettelivre.co.uk

The Sandbag Secret

by Jon Blake
Illustrations by Martin Remphry

FRANKLIN WATTS
LONDON•SYDNEY

1

The Secret Cabinet

It stood in the corner of the room. Just a
cheap wooden cabinet, two foot wide by
three foot tall. It was there when I came
back from the country after being evacuated.

The cabinet was owned by my Uncle
Sandy, who had taken over my room while

I was away. I had never seen him open it and there was always a padlock on the door.

We called Uncle Sandy *Uncle Sandbag* because that's what he was like. Short, round and difficult to budge. You could sometimes fire questions at him all day and you wouldn't get an answer.

Well, I was determined to get one answer. I was determined to find out what was in that cabinet.

It was September 1940. Around our table sat seven people – Mum, Dad, me (Billy), my sister Ruby, my brother Roy, Grandad, and Uncle Sandbag.

"What's for tea, Mum?" I asked, cheerfully.

"Woolton Pie," replied Mum.

My heart sank.

"Not Woolton Pie again!" I groaned.

"Shut up and eat what you're given," said Dad.

We'd had some weird food since rationing started. Dried egg omelettes, soya bean dumplings, and this stuff which looked like meat, tasted of fish, and turned out to be whale. None was quite as bad as Woolton Pie, which was made of parsnips, turnips and other things so disgusting they had to be hidden under pastry.

Not that we had better food before the war. Dad was unemployed and we lived in the poorest part of London, the East End. Things were always hard for us.

"I'll have the boy's pie if he doesn't want it," said Uncle Sandbag.

"I *do* want it!" I cried quickly.

That was typical of Uncle Sandbag. The government had a campaign called Dig for Victory which encouraged people to grow their own veg. Uncle Sandbag had his own campaign called Pig for Victory, which involved eating everyone else's food and never sharing his own.

"What did your sister say in her letter, Mildred?" asked Dad.

"She says Portsmouth's had a terrible pounding," replied Mum.

"Do you think they'll bomb London?" asked Ruby, nervously.

"Not unless they're mad!" I said. I told everyone what Gassy Cook had told me. London's air defences were unbeatable – fighter planes, anti-aircraft guns, barrage balloons, you name it.

"But Hitler *is* mad," said Ruby.

"We should never have bombed Berlin," said Grandad.

That was typical of Grandad. Always questioning what the government did.

Grandad used to be a big union man down the docks and Mum said he was red in tooth and claw, whatever that meant.

After tea Ruby went off for her night shift at the weapons factory. Mum sent me on a mission down the road to borrow some cocoa from Mrs Frost.

On the way I passed a new poster by the corner shop.

LOOK OUT - THERE'S A SPY ABOUT.

I studied this poster a long time. The picture showed a man who looked like an ordinary city gent. He didn't have a peculiar hat or funny moustache and he didn't carry a bomb. In other words, he could be anybody. That was a worrying thought.

When I got back from my walk I went up to my room to find Uncle Sandbag struggling with his socks.

"Get these off for me,
will you, Billy?" he said.

"Do I have to?" I replied.

Uncle Sandbag's feet would have
knocked out a gorilla. I don't know why
they stank so bad. Maybe it was the long
walks he went on every day. No one knew
exactly where he went, or what he did.
Uncle Sandbag just said he had "business".

I squatted down by Uncle Sandbag's feet. Then I had a great idea. I took the gas mask out of my shoulder bag and put it on.

Uncle Sandbag didn't see the funny side at all.

"You won't laugh," he said, "when you're using that mask for real."

Uncle Sandbag sounded very sure of this. It was as if he knew something that the rest of us didn't.

2

The Sirens Sound

Next day was Saturday, the 7th of
September. It started like any other day.
We did some queuing, then some more
queuing, then a bit more queuing.

Shopping in wartime was a real pain.
Once I suggested to Dad that we should

buy things off the black market, but he went mad. Only scum dealt on the black market, he said, when everyone else was doing without.

Anyway, that afternoon, when the shopping was done, there came a sound we had hoped never to hear – the wail of the air-raid sirens.

For a while we just stood, staring at the calm afternoon sky, wondering if there'd been a mistake. Then we had the shock of our lives. Over in the east, the sky was turning black with German bombers.

"Inside!" hissed Dad.

The next few hours were the most frightening of my life. The whole family crouched beneath the dinner table, with a mattress on top and armchairs overturned around the sides.

Outside it sounded like the end of the world – an endless racket of explosions and anti-aircraft fire, most of it so close we jumped for shock.

"Why don't they go and bomb the
rich?" growled Grandad.

Eventually there was a break in the
bombing. We looked out to see that
several of the houses in our street had been
hit, and the whole landscape was lit by the
fearsome glow of the burning docks.

But it wasn't over yet. The docks made a lovely bright beacon for the night bombers, and soon we were crouched back under the table, more terrified than ever. Only Grandad remained calm.

"Of course," he said, in his best story-telling voice, "I remember the *last* time we had Nazis in the East End."

"What?" I said. "Hitler's been here before?"

"Not Hitler," said Grandad. "These were British Nazis. Except they weren't really Nazis. They were called the British Union of Fascists and they were led by a man called Mosley."

"The blackshirts," chimed Dad. "I remember them."

"What happened to them?" I asked.

"We sent them packing," said Grandad.

"Wow!" I said. "Was there a fight?"

"You could say that," said Grandad.
"Half the East End turned out to kick their
backsides. Mosley made it as far as Cable
Street, then we broke through the police
lines, and all hell let loose. It was the
beginning of the end for Mosley."

"Are there any of these Nazis still about?" I asked, nervously.

"Most got locked up when the war started," replied Grandad. "But I dare say there's still a few roaming free."

I suddenly became aware of Uncle Sandbag's foot nudging me in my ribs. He had gone very quiet. Even in the gloom I could see the cagey look on his face.

3

In Search of a Spy

There was no doubt in my mind now. Uncle Sandbag was a Nazi. I could just imagine him in one of those black shirts, goose-stepping like we'd seen in the newsreels.

And if Uncle Sandbag was a Nazi, it was a dead cert that he was also. . . a spy!

So that's what this "business" was all about! Spying on the British defences, then radioing back to Germany!

But where did he keep his radio set? Of course! The bedroom cabinet!

I made up my mind to follow Uncle Sandbag next day. If I could stop him, I reckoned I might just save London.

The moment Uncle Sandbag set off, I followed on my bicycle, a safe distance behind. The stench of burning rubber and God-knows-what was still hanging in the air. Destruction was everywhere, and most of it was just ordinary people's homes. Rescue workers still sifted through the rubble, looking dog-tired and filthy.

Uncle Sandbag was a man with a mission. He strode out like a marching soldier, casting glances left and right, but never hesitating for a moment.

He turned into a side street. I hurried after,
then jammed on the brakes. The street had
been cordoned off
because of an
unexploded bomb.
Uncle Sandbag
was turning back.

I cycled furiously to the next street and hid behind the end wall of a flattened terrace. Uncle Sandbag marched past, fortunately with his eyes straight ahead. Then, just as I was about to give chase, I heard a faint, faint human groan from beneath the rubble.

What could I do? Uncle Sandbag was getting away, but I couldn't ignore the poor soul beneath me. I rode as fast as I could to the warden's post three streets away and blurted out that somebody was buried alive.

Wearily the warden grabbed his hat.

We picked up volunteers along the way and were soon digging into the piles of rafters, brick, plaster and glass that used to be a house.

The groaning seemed to have stopped.

"I should stay clear," said the warden, "if you've never seen a dead body."

Dead body? I was horrified. But I had to watch. The rescue workers turned over the remains of a chair and a leg came into view. Then another . . . then a body, arms, and finally a white, white face, caked in plaster and covered in little red gashes from broken glass.

Suddenly I realised. It was the face of Mr Sanders, who taught at our school!

I watched numbly as they lifted him carefully out, lifeless as a dummy. Then, just as they carried him past me, his white-caked eyes opened. He looked straight at me, confused and blurred.

"Billy Harvey?" he murmured.

"Yes, Sir," I replied, as if he were taking register.

I just hoped my mates never found out I'd saved a teacher.

Mr Stokes the warden congratulated me when the rescue was over. He said I could make a useful messenger boy for the air raid patrol. I said I'd think about it. I couldn't tell him I was on a more important mission.

"He was lucky to be alive," said Mr Stokes. "We pulled out a whole family last time. All dead. It's no darn good hiding under a table if a bomb comes through your blasted roof."

"Wh-what do you think people should do?" I asked.

"Get an Anderson shelter," said Mr Stokes. "And if you ain't got an Anderson, get out of the East End."

We hadn't got an Anderson shelter. According to Gassy Cook, an Anderson shelter was a load of corrugated iron which the council delivered  to your front door. You dug a hole in the back garden and sunk it there. According to Gassy Cook, it then filled with water and you sat there knee-deep all night. But at least you had a chance of surviving if a bomb hit your house.

I decided I wanted to survive.

"Mum," I said, as soon as I got home, "I think we should move."

"Don't be silly," said Mum.

Mum really believed the government would protect us if the bombers came again. But I was starting to agree with Grandad. The government didn't really care if we lived or died.

"Is Uncle back?" I asked, changing the subject.

"Yes," said Mum. "He's been up in the bedroom for ages."

I was off like a rocket up the stairs. Maybe this time I'd catch him.

No such luck. Uncle Sandbag was calmly sitting on the bed reading a newspaper.

He gave me a little smile which convinced
me he'd just radioed Germany. That's it,
I thought to myself. The bombers will be
back tonight.

4

Caught in the Act

I wasn't wrong. The second night of
bombing was every bit as bad as the first.
Once again the East End copped it, and if
anything, our anti-aircraft fire was even
weaker. It even crossed my mind that Nazi
spies were manning the guns.

By morning we were shattered. But it was Monday, and that meant work, and school. If you didn't go to work, you didn't get paid, and if you didn't go to school, you got ten good stripes from Mr Morgan's cane.

The playground was buzzing with stories and souvenirs. Jimmy Hayes had shrapnel, Tommy Jacobs had cartridge cases, and Harold Green had this long metal tube. Mr Morgan got very excited

about this and shouted "You Stupid Boy". He said it was an incendiary bomb – that's the type that starts fires. The only fire Harold felt was the one in the seat of his pants from Mr Morgan's cane.

For all the big talk, you could tell kids were shaken by things they'd seen. When the register was taken, every time someone was missing, it went very quiet. Still, we could always pretend they'd just moved away, or got injured, like Mr Sanders.

Halfway through the afternoon the sirens went, and we all filed down to the school shelter. I took the chance to tell Gassy Cook all about Uncle Sandbag, his suspicious behaviour, and his mysterious cabinet.

As always, Gassy had the answer. "I'll pick the lock," he said.

"Can you pick locks?" I asked.

"Sure I can!"

So it was that Gassy followed me home that afternoon. We told Mum I was helping Gassy with his homework, then tiptoed up to the bedroom.

Good news. No sign of uncle. I kept watch through a little hole in the blackout and Gassy got to work.

"Hmm" he said. "Nothing special."

Gassy took out a thin piece of wire, poked it in the keyhole and felt around a bit.

"Shouldn't take a minute."

Unfortunately Gassy was wrong. It took several minutes, and still he wasn't getting anywhere.

"Are you *sure* you know how to pick locks?" I asked.

"Course!"

Time wore on. I became nervous.

"Tell you what," said Gassy, "I'll try another way."

With that, Gassy whipped out a screwdriver and started undoing the whole lock. It would look the same when he was done, he said.

The screws began to loosen and my stomach began to tighten.

Suddenly there was a footfall on the stair. Not Grandad's – too heavy for that. Not Dad's – he'd gone to volunteer as a firefighter.

I held my breath.

Then the door flew open and my worst nightmare came true.

"What the hell are you doing!?"

I had never seen Uncle Sandbag look so frightening. The veins on his neck bulged and his eyes were aflame with fury.

"We wanted . . . to borrow some screws," I said, lamely.

Uncle Sandbag swiftly shut the door, then took one great stride into the room, snatching the screwdriver from Gassy and covering the cabinet with his big baggy body.

"Have you opened this?" he stormed.

"No, Uncle, honest!"

"What have you seen?" he snapped.

"Nothing! Nothing!"

Both Gassy and I were crouched in terror on the bed. I was sure Uncle Sandbag had a gun in that strange case he always carried. Or maybe a knife in his belt. Either way, he looked ready to kill us.

"You listen to me!" he said.

"That cabinet's mine, and everything inside it! *No one else's!* Understand?"

"Yes, Uncle" I replied meekly.

There was no way I'd risk touching that cabinet again.

5

A Race For Safety

And that might have been the end of the
story. I might have been none the wiser
about Uncle Sandbag. But it wasn't the
end of the Blitz, far from it, and that night
the bombers were back. Ruby was working,
Dad was with the firefighters, and the rest

of us were back under the kitchen table.

Then, suddenly, there was an almighty BOOM like the Earth had cracked.

"They've hit us!" yelled Mum.

We sat stock still in shock. You could smell the fear, and most of it seemed to be in my brother Roy's shorts.

"Must be next door," said Grandad, noticing that we were all still alive.

Suddenly Mum started pushing us out from under the table. "Come on!" she said.

"Where are we going?" I asked.

"Somewhere safe," said Mum.

There was no time to take anything with us. The whole family was bundled out of the front door, right into the middle of the most terrible sound-and-light show you could imagine. Searchlights swept the sky, anti-aircraft shells exploded in the air, giant bombers droned overhead, and the

whole landscape was lit by fires and explosions. It almost seemed unreal, but the danger of death was real enough.

We ran through the streets, hardly daring to stop for breath. We knew there were shelters, but we had no idea what we'd find there. Some said the shelters were no safer than your own home, and that you'd be lucky to find one with a roof. Others said they were like visions of hell, thousands of people crammed together and not one toilet.

As we reached the main road, however, we could see there was one place to shelter we hadn't thought of – the underground station. There was a crowd of people there, and as we got closer we could see a line of troops holding them back. The atmosphere was dangerous and panicky and tempers were frayed.

A railway official was frantically pointing at a poster on the wall:

UNDERGROUND STATIONS MUST NOT BE USED AS AIR RAID SHELTERS.

But whatever the reasons the man was giving, they weren't going down well with the East Enders. The crowd surged, the troops pushed back, and Grandad took us smartly to one side.

"Has everyone got three ha'pence?"
he asked.

We nodded.

"Follow me," said Grandad. He made
his way past the edge of the crowd to the
ticket office, bought a ticket, and set off
down to the trains. We followed. Reaching
the platform, Grandad selected a nice spot
and sat himself down.

"Now try and move me," he said.

51

Soon dozens more were copying Grandad's example. The platform was starting to look like a street party. I looked on enviously as other families arrived with blankets, flasks and sandwiches.

It was a strange and magical atmosphere down in that tube station. Everybody got talking, and of course we'd all been through the same things.

Soon people were sharing the few things
they'd got – cushions, cigarettes,
sandwiches. It really made you feel you
belonged. You were an East Ender.

Uncle Sandbag, on the other hand,
seemed to find all this very difficult. He sat
at a distance from everybody else and kept
himself to himself.

Needless to say, people noticed.

"Wouldn't your uncle like a nice hot cup of tea?" asked the woman next to me, "or a sandwich?"

Uncle Sandbag half turned. I knew he was starving, and like I said, his motto was Pig for Victory.

"Sandwich, love?" asked the woman. "We're all in the same boat."

Suddenly Uncle Sandbag jumped to his feet. "I've forgotten something," he mumbled. Without another word he marched back up the steps towards the surface.

"Sandy!" cried Mum. "Where are you going?"

But there was no further sign of Uncle Sandbag.

6

A Guilty Surprise

The next thing I remember was being elbowed in the ribs by my brother.

"Come on, Bill," he said. "The all-clear's gone."

I rubbed my eyes and looked around. "Where's Uncle Sandbag?" I asked.

"He never came back," replied my brother.

We made our way back up the steps, past the ticket office, and into the light. Things were quiet now, apart from the occasional ambulance. We sloped back home, wondering what we would find.

Just as we were about to turn our corner, Mrs Harrison from across the road rushed over to Mum and put her arms round her.

"Mildred!" she said. "We thought you were under the rubble."

"What rubble?" said Mum, almost silently.

"But didn't you know? You were hit last night."

I had strange mixed feelings of relief and sickness.

"We thought you were all under there," said Mrs Harrison, "once they found the first body."

A chill went through me. Uncle Sandbag!

Suddenly we found ourselves running, down a street we hardly recognised, to a house which no longer existed. The warden showed us the spot they dug out our uncle.

There, amongst the bricks and rafters,
lay a certain small cabinet,
the door blasted
from its hinges.

I gasped. The cabinet was stuffed with
every foodstuff you could imagine – butter,
tins of fruit, sugar, flour, even chocolate.
There were fags as well.

"I think someone's been working the
black market," said the warden, sternly.

"We knew nothing," said Mum, stunned.

"Funny thing," said the warden, "but
his pockets were filled with the stuff as well.
Must have been on his way somewhere."

Yes, I thought. Back to the tube, to share it out with the rest of the people there.

For all the bad things I'd thought about Uncle Sandbag, I knew that was what he was doing.

"Is he. . . dead?" I asked.

The warden looked at me long and hard. "Not till I get my hands on him," he replied.

"I'll be right behind you," said Mum.

I said nothing. I remembered Grandad saying there was a little bit of good in everyone.

Looked like the Blitz had finally brought it out of Uncle Sandbag.

London at War

The Blitz

The Blitz got its
name from "Blitzkrieg" –
German for "lightning war". This described
how quickly countries were attacked and how
much damage was done to them.

Mass bombing first took place in the Spanish
Civil War. In 1937, 43 planes dropped 100,000
tonnes of explosives on the town of Guernica.
The world was shocked. Some people began to
believe that wars would be won by bombing cities
rather than fighting.

A Surprise Attack

The Blitz began on 7 September 1940 and ended
on 10 May 1941. London was bombed for 76

nights in a row, apart from just one night. About 43,000 people died; two million homes were damaged or destroyed; one and a half million people were made homeless.

The government did not expect the Blitz. The shelters they provided were unsafe, unclean and too few in number. The main targets were homes and factories. When factories were hit, they stopped producing goods. This meant there was a shortage of everyday things like soap, clothes and food. Hitler wanted to make the British people give up hope by destroying their homes and cutting off supplies. However, people's spirits did not collapse as badly as Hitler hoped.

Pick up a SPARKS to read exciting tales of what life was really like for ordinary people.